BMX Winners

A Fact and Fiction Book
by
Ed and Ruth Radlauer

AN ELK GROVE BOOK

CP CHILDRENS PRESS ™

CHICAGO

Created for Childrens Press
by Radlauer Productions, Incorporated

For help with the manuscript, the authors thank Keith Davis, Irvine, California, and Robin Radlauer, San Diego.

Photographs taken at BMX tracks sanctioned by the American Bicycle Association.

Photo Credits:
Pages 20 and 30 by Robin Radlauer

Type for this book was transferred electronically from a Kaypro II and Signalman modem in La Habra Heights, California, to a Compugraphic® Typesetter at Stephens Printing Company in Glendale, California.

Library of Congress Cataloging in Publication Data

Radlauer, Ed.
    BMX winners.

    (Fact and fiction books)
    "An Elk Grove book."
    Includes index.
    Summary: With the help of the new girl member, Pete and the rest of the Spooky Spokes racing team learn that it takes more than good equipment to win on the track. Includes a glossary of terms.
    1. Children's stories, American. [1. Bicycle motocross—Fiction. 2. Bicycle racing—Fiction]
I. Radlauer, Ruth, 1926-   II. Title. III. Title: B.M.X. winners.
PZ7.R1218BM 1984   [Fic]   84-7818
ISBN 0-516-07813-5   AACR2

Fact and Fiction Books

BMX Winners
Guide Dog Winners
Karting Winners
Minibike Winners
Motorcycle Winners
Soap Box Winners

BMX. That stands for **Bicycle Motocross**, a great sport. This book tells how a racing team called The Spooky Spokes learns that it takes more than good **equipment** to be a winner.

*Words printed **bold face like this** are found in the Index on page 47. Meanings for most of them are found in the Glossary, page 44.

4

The bicycle motocross races were going badly for Pete Davidson. Pete gave his **Mongoose*** BMX bike all he had, but it wasn't enough for this **moto**. He was stuck in the middle of the **pack** and couldn't get out. His start at the beginning had been slow. He'd had trouble holding his balance, waiting for the **gate** to drop. Yes, the new **chrome-moly** handlebars felt good. And the helmet he'd gotten when his older brother quit racing felt good, too. Was he stuck here because he **slipped his pedal** in the second turn? The bad start? No. There was more wrong than that.

"So here I am," Pete said to himself, "captain of the Spooky Spokes bicycle motocross racing team and I can't even **place**. It looks like we'll never get the **points** we need to get into the Team Trophy Championship **Finals**."

The other Spooky Spokes riders hadn't done much good riding, either. "We used to hold **one, two, three, and four** in the **standings**," Pete remembered. "Then we fell behind. The guys just don't seem to care." Pete wondered what he could do to get the Spokes members back in shape.

Pete had good reasons to feel discouraged. Rick Weltoff, one of the Spooky Spokes riders, had

---

Words printed bold face like this are found in the Index on page **47**. Meanings for most of them are found in the Glossary, page **44**.

During a race, there's plenty of action on the turns. Some
riders say you can go faster on the **outside**. Then you have
to use the **berm**. Winning riders go through a turn without
putting a foot down. When you put a foot down, you can't
pedal and that means you lose speed. By the time you get
your foot back on the pedal, you'll find yourself at the
back of the pack.

blown a tube in his moto and dropped out after being in second place. Tony Florio had lost, too. The team's best rider had his chain come off the **sprocket** in the first turn. Brad Mason, who used to place quite a bit, had been **disqualified** for being late to the **staging area**.

Now in this race, right before the final turn, a rider squeezed Pete to the outside. The squeeze was so tight that he almost went over the berm and off the track.

As the moto ended, Pete said to himself, "Last place. I guess that's what I deserved. And wow! That was some rider that almost pushed me off the track. Wonder who *that* was." He headed for the team's **pit area** to wait for the other members to come from the **spectator area**. He'd had it with BMX. Pete pulled his foot back and gave the Mongoose a fast kick.

"Ooo, that's gruesome," said a girl's voice. Pete turned. It was Deena Rossi, Brad Mason's cousin. She was spending the summer with Brad's family because her parents were away. And now he recognized the shirt. This was the rider who had squeezed him into the berm. The shirt read, *Lancaster Lions BMX Team*. Lancaster was about 30 miles from Valley Dunes where the Spokes raced.

No matter how a good a rider you are, you won't win at
BMX if you have **equipment failure**. To win, you need to
have all the parts of your bike in top working condition.
The chain and **axle nuts** are important. In this story, a
rider finds out you can't do much racing if your chain
comes off the sprocket.

Deena had been riding **independent** during the time she was with Brad's family.

Deena went on. "You Spokes didn't place at all, did you? Sure looks like those guys in the Ground Grippers are going to the Team Trophy Championship Finals, huh?"

"So we had some bad luck," Pete answered. "I think you could call it equipment failure. Happens all the time. Just wait, next week—"

"Looks to me like the Spooky Spokes haven't won in a long time," Deena said. "And you can't win by using fancy words like 'equipment failure.' That won't get you any points. Your team needs someone to get the riders back into **competition**, someone to show them how to race, how to go wheel-to-wheel, how to—"

"My brother coached us. Well, at least he coached us until he went off to work at that summer camp. He was a champion, too." If only his brother would just come back!

Deena shook her head. "It's got to be more than coaching. You need a member who'll make that old **competitive** spirit come out to work in the races."

Pete stared at Deena. "Do I hear you saying what I think you're saying?"

"Sure! I'd be great on your team. And besides,

Other parts of the bike to check are the chain, **tire pressure**, spokes, **handlebar nut**, and brake. You do the work of checking your bike in the pit area. Now, how can you tell who the winners are? Just look around. Some people spend their time in the pits talking to friends. Others spend some time working on their bikes. Which ones do you think are the winners?

it's no fun riding independent here all summer."

Pete was about to tell Deena to get lost. But he thought for a moment. Maybe this wasn't such a goofy idea. Somehow it seemed to make sense. Could having someone like Deena Rossi on the Spokes' team get the riders back to feeling competitive? It might be worth a try. Right about now, *anything* seemed worth a try.

"Well, what do you say?"

"I kind of like the idea. Only I don't know about the other riders. Some of them will vote a loud NO!" Pete yelled the "NO!" so loudly that people in the pits turned and stared.

Deena turned to the people around them. She shrugged her shoulders and calmly announced, "All I did was ask him to marry me."

It was the Tuesday after race day. Pete and the three other Spooky Spokes members were in the Davidson garage. Pete sat on the workbench holding a big hammer, the **official** team gavel. "This meeting is officially open," Pete said and banged the hammer on the workbench. "Everyone here say, 'Present.' "

The other team members, who were half standing, half sitting on their bikes all mumbled, "Present."

Before each race, riders gather in the staging area behind the starting line. The **stager** calls the numbers of the riders in each **class** for the next race. If your number is called twice and you don't show up, you are out of the race. You and your team will get no points. The Spooky Spokes riders find out that's not so good if your team is trying to win.

Rick Weltoff spoke up. "How come we're having this meeting, anyway?"

"Yeah," Brad Mason agreed. "How come?"

"I gotta do my paper route," Tony Florio added.

"You'll get to your paper route," Pete said. "But we're having this meeting because we have to take care of official Spooky Spokes business."

"What's that?" Rick asked.

"Come on, you guys," Tony argued. "Let's get done with the business, huh?"

"Right," Pete said. "Now our first business is bad news. All the other teams, especially the Ground Grippers, are picking up points and leaving us in the dust. If we don't start placing, it's goodbye to the Championship Finals for us. What's wrong with our team? Like you, Brad. Disqualified for being late in the staging area."

"I knew it was my moto. But I got to talking to someone and I didn't hear the **call**."

"Then you must have been talking an awful lot," Pete said. "The stager called your class twice, just like always. Don't you remember how my brother always told us to get into the staging area way ahead of the call?"

"Yeah, I remember," Brad said, "only this time I forgot and—"

To do **tabletops**, you need to have you *and* your bike in good shape. Doing tabletops is fun for riders and spectators. But in a race, you won't see many tabletops because good riders go through jumps at the best possible speed. They know doing fancy tricks slows them down.

Pete banged the hammer. "That's only part of what's wrong. Brad misses a moto, Tony loses his chain, and Rick blows a tube."

"Yeah, it was my new **ultra light**, too," Rick added.

"I know how come you blew it," Tony Florio said. "You didn't check your tire pressure. Remember how we learned that pressure goes up when you start to race? You're supposed to use a **tire gauge**."

"So I didn't have one."

"You could always borrow one from—"

Pete banged the hammer. "Listen, you guys. Arguing isn't getting us any points. We've got to take care of our bikes. Check them before each moto." He banged the hammer once more. "Someone make a motion that team rules say you have to check your bike before each moto."

Tony spoke up. "I move that."

Pete held up the hammer. "All in favor?"

Three voices yelled, "Aye."

Pete banged the hammer once more. "Motion passed."

"Quit it with the hammer, and are we finished?" Tony asked. "I'm gonna be late for my paper route."

"So what?" Rick said. "No one reads the dumb

Most people who go into BMX racing belong to an
association. Associations set the rules that keep the races
fair and safe. Some associations have special classes for
girls. Others say boys and girls can race in the same class
at the same time. Association rules also tell how the track
is to be set up, what ages people must be for certain
classes, and how points will be scored.

TRIBUNE anyway. My dad just uses it to light the barbeque fire."

"Come on, you guys," Pete ordered. "We've got more official business. What else can we do to keep the Grippers from beating us? We used to place all the time. If we start winning again we still have a chance."

"How about you?" Tony asked. "You let a rider almost run you off the track on the final turn. And it was a girl."

"That wasn't a girl," Brad said. "That was my Cousin Deena."

"And that's our next official business," Pete announced. "We have someone who wants to join the Spooky Spokes."

"I vote no!" Brad yelled.

"How can you vote no when you don't even know who it is?" Tony asked.

"Because it's my cousin, that's why," Brad answered.

"A girl? On our team?" Tony whacked himself on the side of the head. "I vote no. I vote no twice. Besides the **ABA** puts girls in their own class."

"The rules say girls can ride in the boys' **intermediate classes.**" Rick argued. "And what's

Part of your racing equipment might be a special racing shirt. The shirt could tell if you belong to a team or have a **sponsor**. Since good BMX bikes and equipment are very expensive, many riders like to have sponsors. Also, if you belong to a team, such as the Spooky Spokes or Ground Grippers in the story, you want people to know about it. Riders are proud of their team shirts, especially when their team wins.

wrong with Brad's cousin? Didn't she win last week? And the week before that she took second."

"So what!" Brad said. "Listen, if she gets to be on this team, she'll be telling us what to do all the time just like she does at home. She'd be worse than Pete with his stupid hammer. Tell her to join the Grippers. That should give them—"

"First place!" Pete shouted as he banged the hammer.

"Quit it!" Tony yelled back. "And I vote NO!"

"And I vote yes," Pete said. "How about you, Rick?"

"Sure, let her in. I'll ask my mom to make her a Spooky Spokes racing shirt."

"Not so fast," Brad argued. "I vote no. That makes it two and two. A tie."

"Yeah, a tie. That means she's not in," Tony said.

"I say she's in," Rick argued. "What do you say, Pete, you're captain. You're supposed to know everything."

Pete remembered how he hoped Deena would make the members competitive again. He'd have to do something to get her on the team. Still, he didn't want to get Tony Florio so mad he'd quit the team.

There are many ways to win a race. There are also many
ways to lose a race. Having your equipment fail is a way to
lose. Making a good start is a help if you want to win.
Riders make good starts by balancing their bikes with the
front wheels against the starting gate. When the starter
says, "Riders ready, watch the **white lines**," it's time to
GO!

"Okay, so we voted a tie. Deena isn't on the team or off the team. I say let's take her on as a trial rider because my brother once told us that a team needs someone who can tell them what they're doing right or wrong."

"Deena will do that all day long, you bet," Brad said.

Pete waved the hammer. "If it helps and we start beating the Grippers, so what? Then she can stay. If not, she'll just have to go back to riding independent or find herself another team."

Everyone mumbled. Then Tony said, "Okay, but she better be good or I'm quitting the Spokes. I'll be your enemy. I'll ride for the Ground Grippers."

"Oh, go peddle your papers," Rick said. "My dad needs one to light the barbeque fire."

Pete banged the hammer. "The meeting's over until Friday after school when we bring Deena Rossi in as a trial rider on the Spooky Spokes Team."

On Friday afternoon Deena came to the meeting of the Spooky Spokes BMX team. Pete started by saying, "I told Deena she could be a trial member and she said it was okay. Now let's get busy figuring out what to do on race day. If we don't place this time, we're out of the the Championship Finals for sure."

On your BMX bike, the handlebars are used for more than steering. You'll use them when you make a jump. In the story, you find out that the angle of the handlebars has to be just right or your jump may go just wrong. Padding on the handlebars and **frame** is important so you won't wreck yourself in case you **munch it**.

Deena spoke up. "You guys lost last time because your bikes fell apart and one rider missed a moto."

"*Come on*, Deena, I only lost a chain," Tony said. "My bike didn't *fall* apart."

"Sure," Deena agreed. "You lost a chain because you didn't check to see if your axle nut was tight. That meant you didn't place. Rick blows a tube. More bad news. We've all got to make sure our bikes are in top shape, all checked."

Tony Florio laughed. "We decided that for ourselves at the last meeting. We even passed a motion. So what else is new? Our team doesn't need *you* to tell us that."

"What did I tell you guys, huh?" Brad put in. "Boss, boss. Deena's got a big mouth."

Deena ignored her cousin. "Checking your own bike isn't good enough. You get so used to your own bike you can't see what's wrong. You have to check *each other's* bikes. That's how we do it in the Lancaster Lions where I usually race." Deena pointed at Tony's bike. "Look, see Tony's handlebars? They're at the wrong angle for racing."

"I got to keep them that way so I can carry my papers," Tony said. "I don't have money for a

Riding style is the way a person rides. Some riders get
very competitive, push their way ahead. Others sort of
hang back and don't try quite as hard. A rider's style
shows up at all parts of the track, but especially in the
turns, where the competition is hardest. In the story, you
find out if the Spooky Spokes are competitive or not.

thrasher bike *and* a **custom job**, like some other people I know."

"Then you better move your handlebars for race day, or your jumps are going to look like you've got your wheels nailed to the dirt."

"That sounds funny," Pete said.

"See?" Brad said. "More bossing, like I told you."

"If it helps us win, then it's okay with me," Rick said. "Anything wrong with my bike?"

"Not if you get back to riding like a real **competitor**," Deena answered. Then she added, "That goes for all of you."

"What's that supposed to mean?" Rick asked.

"It's simple," Deena answered. "Use some psychological warfare. Get out and scare the other riders right off—"

Pete banged the hammer. "We know what Deena means. And I like that psychological warfare idea. It means riding like we did when we were winners. Okay all of you, be on time for race day. Maybe we'll get back **in the running** for the Championship Finals."

"Hey, Pete," Tony said. "How's about you bang your psychological hammer one more time and tell us the meeting is officially over. I gotta deliver my papers. Lots of people have their barbeques on Friday night."

BMX racing bikes have very lightweight, very strong frames. Bicycle parts, such as front forks and pedals, are mounted on the frame. Even the rider mounts on the frame!

"Yeah, sure," Pete agreed. Things were looking better. Maybe having Deena on the team would make the members more competitive. Well, they'd soon find out.

On race day, the five members of the Spooky Spokes BMX team set up their pit area. They chose a place that was off from the rest of the racers so they could work on their secret psychological warfare plan.

The Spokes members grinned at each other when some riders from the Ground Grippers came by and stopped. Frankie Lester, one of the Grippers, said, "How come you guys want to be way off here by yourselves? Have you *Kookie* Spokes got a secret weapon? A new kind of frame or something?"

Tony stood up. He'd been adjusting his chain. Wrench in hand, Tony pointed at Deena. "Yeah, we got a new weapon. I'm pointing at it, and Frankie Lester, you better be careful what you say. It'll bite your head off, especially if you keep calling us *Kookie* Spokes."

Frankie laughed. "Deena on your team? Now you guys are *really* Kookie. Just wait. Out there on the track we'll make you eat our dust."

Deena spoke up. "Now listen, *Gruesome*, after

Before the races start, riders have **practice time** on the track. Good riders know practice is important. It's the time you have to get the feel of the track. Practice time is when you find the places on the track where it's good to pedal, use the brakes, or pass somebody.

today, people are going to wonder if you guys need training wheels on your bikes." Deena turned to Pete. "Let's not waste any time with these *Gruesome Grippers*."

The riders from the Ground Grippers walked away and the Spooky Spokes members laughed.

"Our plan may work, huh?" Rick asked.

"Yeah," Pete answered. "It's like Deena said. First we get them mad in the pits and then we bug them on the track. I think psychological warfare is going to work for us."

Tony added, "Maybe we'll have to rename our team the Psychological Spokes, right?"

"Naw, that would never work," Brad said.

"Oh yeah? And why not?" Tony asked.

"Because none of us knows how to spell *psychological*."

An official announced practice time and the five Spooky Spokes riders lined up at the starting gate with the other teams. The track was open and practice started. Rick, Tony, and Brad were set to follow certain Ground Gripper riders. "Remember what we planned," Pete instructed. "Get close to them. Ride wheel-to-wheel. Don't get off their tails for a minute. Watch how they ride. Try to figure ways to get out in front of them."

Very good riders use practice time to watch the
competitors. Some riders use this time to set up a race plan
against certain riders whom they need to beat. In this story,
the Spooky Spokes team uses practice time in a very
special way.

"Right!" Deena agreed. "And while you're doing that, Pete and I will ride and watch for things we can do when the motos start."

As practice time went on, Rick, Brad, and Tony found the riders they were to follow and signaled to each other. Tony rode handlebar-to-handlebar with the rider he'd been following and yelled, "Hey, Gruesome, you better watch out for us Kookie Spooks."

Pete and Deena kept toward the back. They studied riders who'd be the competition for the Spokes. For the first time in weeks, Pete had a good time on the track. He watched Frankie Lester to see where he might leave room on the track for a rider to pass him. Good thing he'd talked the team members into taking Deena in as a trial member. Now they might have a chance at the Finals.

Deena yelled to Pete, "This turn is a good place to make your move."

Pete nodded. Deena had almost run him off the track on this turn during the race a week ago. "Might be a good place to pull that same trick, if I need it," he thought.

Practice ended and the Spokes headed for their pit area. No one could see the grins behind the **rock guards** that covered the faces of the Spooky Spokes riders.

Some say the start of a race is the most exciting part. It may be exciting, but it's also important. It's time for you to be standing up on your bike, balanced, front wheel against the gate, and pedals in **power position**. Every muscle in your body also needs to be ready for a quick start. Good riders know it's much easier to *stay* ahead in a race than to *get* ahead when you've fallen behind.

Pete called one more meeting before the races started. They all made a huddle and did a lot of low talking. Every once in a while one of the members turned and pointed at a rider on the Ground Grippers team. From their huddle, they could see some worried-looking Ground Grippers. The psychological warfare might be working. Each rider had a racing plan, and now for the test.

Because the class was so big, the Spokes team and the Ground Grippers were in three different sets of races. Deena and Brad were in the first moto. Tony and Rick raced together in the second moto. And Pete was the only Spokes rider in the third moto. "I guess we have our work cut out for us," Pete said. "We all race against some of the Grippers. I get to take on Frankie Lester."

"If our plans work," Deena said, "we'll beat the Grippers, even big-shot Frankie Lester."

The **track director** announced the start of the races. About one hundred riders in many different classes pushed their bikes to the staging area.

Finally the first moto riders lined up at the starting line. Deena and Brad were two and three out of the gate. Deena tailed the rider in first place and then, in her favorite turn, she made a move and took over first. Brad tried, but didn't have the power to take second. He had to settle for third.

Now, that's bad news, a munch. What causes a munch? You can munch it if you make a very sharp turn. Or if you get yourself tangled with another rider. You'll munch it for sure if you come out of a big jump and **endo**. And there's one more thing. Officials don't give you any points for a munch.

As soon as Deena and Brad were back in the staging area, Pete yelled to them. "Great, you guys! We're picking up points!"

Tony and Rick rode their motos. Tony, the **power rider**, pulled the **hole shot** to get into first place, but Rick had a **two-pedal slip** and fell back to fourth.

In his moto, Pete tailed Frankie Lester, who was in first place. But Frankie was too far ahead to have Pete bother him. "I've got to get closer on my next moto or the psychological warfare isn't going to work," Pete thought.

The Spokes raced on, winning in some motos, losing in others, but still doing better than they had in weeks. In a last huddle before the final moto, Pete talked in a low voice. "Listen, guys, we're doing great. I figure if we can take one first or two seconds in our last motos, we've got the points we need to go on to the Finals. Remember, stick to our plans. Make those Grippers nervous. And the other thing is, being ahead during the race doesn't mean you win. You just have to be ahead at the finish line."

For their last moto, Rick picked up a second and Tony only had a fourth. "Not enough," Pete thought.

From the staging area, Pete watched Deena and

If you are behind but *do* have a race plan, the final turn is where you may have your last chance to *make your move*. From the race plan you worked out during practice, you'll know how your main competitor takes the final turn. Members of the Spooky Spokes racing team used their racing plans to help them come in winners.

Brad. "Great!" he said to himself as he watched them holding one and two. Then there was a gasp from the spectators as Deena munched it in the second turn. Right behind her, Brad slid off the track to keep from piling into his cousin. Neither finished the race.

Pete carefully put his front wheel against the gate and balanced himself for a **two-pedal start**. "Now it's up to me, and I wish my stomach would stop jumping. Maybe it's time to try a little psychological warfare here at the gate." Pete turned to Frankie Lester on his left. "I bet you'll be proud of us Kookie Spokes when we go to the Team Trophy Championship, right Frankie?"

"Huh!" Frankie snorted. "You Kookie Spookies won't talk that way when *this* moto is over."

The gate fell and Frankie took the lead with Pete close behind. Pete gave his Mongoose all he could, but powerful Frankie held on. Then at the last turn, Pete heard Deena scream, "Now, Pete!"

He gave one last super push, went to the inside, and passed Frankie. He heard Frankie close behind. Pete gave his bike all he had and a little bit more. This time it was enough! He had a first! The Spooky Spokes had the points to get into the Finals.

Pete brought his bike to a stop as his team ran

In BMX most people ride independent. They try to get enough points during a **season** so they will be able to get into the very difficult special races where true winners get to race other winners.

over and crowded around him. They pounded him on the back, the shoulders, the helmet. "We did it!" Deena yelled. "Psychological BMX warfare. It blew the Grippers off the track."

On their way back to the pits, Deena, Pete, Rick, Brad, and Tony passed the Ground Grippers' area. All of a sudden, Frankie Lester pulled his foot back and gave his bike a fast kick. The bike skidded across the dirt and crashed against two other bikes.

Pete and Deena looked at each other. "Ooo," Deena said. "That's what I call real *gruesome*."

"Yahoo!" Brad yelled. "*Grue-some* for sure."

It was the Tuesday after the Spooky Spokes had won the points they needed to get into the Team Trophy Championship Finals. All the members waited in Pete's garage for their team captain to start the meeting. "Bang!" went the hammer and Pete said, "This meeting is officially open."

But no one listened. The riders were still talking about how they all scored for their win at Valley Dunes—all except Deena Rossi. She sat quietly off to to the side. Only Pete noticed.

Pete pounded some more and the talking stopped. "This meeting is officially open. Now we have

Yes, there's a lot a rider has to know to be a winner at
bicycle motocross. The Spooky Spokes team learns a lot
about racing in a very short but important time.

two things of official business. One is to plan for the Championship Finals. That's only two weeks off. But first let's have a motion to make Deena a regular member of the Spooky Spokes BMX team."

"I move that!" Tony Florio yelled.

This time there were four loud "AYES!" and one soft "No."

Rick, Pete, Tony, and Brad turned and looked at Deena. "What did you say?" Brad asked.

"You heard me," Deena answered. "I voted no."

"But you still have to be on the team," Rick argued. "The vote was four to one."

"It's still no," Deena insisted. "My parents are coming back in three days. I'm going home to race with the Lancaster Lions. And, just in case you hadn't heard, the Lions are going to be in the Team Trophy Championship Finals, too!"

"Like wow!" Brad said.

"Yeah, like double wow," Rick added.

"So listen carefully," Deena warned. "When the Lions meet the Spokes, it's going to be time to find out who the real BMX winners are when it comes to psychological warfare."

No one spoke. Then Pete banged the hammer. "This meeting's over until later when Deena Rossi isn't

Now you have learned a lot about BMX. Do you think you have what it takes to be a winner in bicycle motocross?

here. We can't plan a race with a Lancaster Lion sitting in."

Pete hammered once more, hard.

Suddenly Tony walked up, stood next to Pete at the workbench, and asked, "Listen, everybody. Do you know what I'm gonna do when the season is over?"

"No, tell us," Pete said.

"I'm gonna take that hammer and use where it will do some good—on a certain captain's head."

"Yeah, right," Rick Weltoff agreed. "Only first let's give a cheer for Deena and her psychological warfare."

"Hooray for Deena and watch out Lancaster Lions!" Brad yelled. "Here come the winning Spooky Spokes."

Pete started to bang the hammer again, but said, "See you guys back here tomorrow afternoon. Like Deena said, two weeks from now we ride in the Team Trophy Championship Finals. That's when we'll find out who the *real* BMX winners are. This meeting is closed." Pete grinned, looked at Tony Florio, and banged the hammer—but not very hard.

Glossary

ABA	**A**merican **B**icycle **A**ssociation—The ABA sets the rules for BMX races. See *association* and *Bicycle Motocross, BMX*.
association	group of people who agree to go by a set of rules
axle	piece of metal that holds the wheel on the frame—See *frame*.
axle nut	metal piece that locks the wheel to the axle—See *axle*.
berm	dirt mound at the edge of the track, usually placed on the outside of the curve
Bicycle Motocross, BMX	bicycle racing held on a dirt track
blow a tube	to have all the air go out of a bicycle tire tube—When this happens, the tire goes flat.
call	announcement telling riders to go to the staging area—See *staging area*.
chrome-moly	metal alloy made by melting steel and adding chromium and molybdenum—Chrome-moly steel is very strong and lightweight.
class	group of riders who race together—A class may be set by rider age, skill, or points won. See *points*.
competition	rider or riders against whom you race
competitive	hard racing, making a big effort to win
competitor	person who does hard racing; person against whom you race
custom job	bicycle made of special parts—Custom parts may include lightweight wheels and frame, racing brakes, and more.
disqualified	put out of the race
endo	hard front wheel landing after a jump—An endo can send a rider flying over the handlebars.
equipment	supplies, parts, or bicycle needed for racing

equipment failure	to have something on a bicycle break
finals	special races to pick top winners
frame	part of a bike on which all other parts are mounted
front forks	place where front wheel is mounted—The handlebar on the front fork controls steering.
gate, starting gate	piece of metal or wood which falls to let the race start—Riders place their front wheels against the gate. To start the race, an official lets the gate drop.
handlebar nut	metal screw-on part that holds the handlebar in place
high turn	curve with dirt stacked very high on the outside
hole shot	to be the first rider to enter the first turn
in the running	having enough points to have a chance to win—See *points*.
independent	not on a team
intermediate class	class between beginners and experts
Mongoose	brand name of a racing bicycle
moto	part of a race—usually once around the track in BMX—See *Bicycle Motocross, BMX*.
munch it	fall while riding a bicycle
official	person who directs the races; important team business
one, two, three, and four	in racing, to come in first, second, third, or fourth
outside	in a curve, away from the center of the track
pack	group of closely spaced riders
pit area, pits	place set aside where people park or work on their bicycles
place, placing	finish a race far enough in the lead to earn points—See *points*.
points	score given for being in first, second, third, or fourth place when a race ends
power position	best position for bicycle pedals for making a good start at the gate—See *gate*.

power rider	rider who has lots of strength
practice time	time set aside to let riders use the track before the races start
rock guard	plastic piece worn to protect the mouth
season	part of the year during which riders collect points—See *points*.
slip a pedal	to have the foot come off a pedal unexpectedly
spectator area	track area from which people watch the races
sponsor	person, club, or company that gives a rider money or equipment for racing—See *equipment*.
sprocket	wheel with points or teeth to drive the chain
stager	official responsible for seeing that the correct riders are in each race—See *official*.
staging area	track area behind starting line where riders wait for their turns to race
standings	points a team or person has compared with other teams or persons
tabletop	high jump on a bicycle which may include right or left turn of the front wheel during the jump—A *tabletop* is a stunt, not part of racing.
team trophy	race where four or five riders accumulate points for their team
thrasher	bicycle used for purposes such as pleasure riding, transportation, paper route
tire gauge	meter to show air pressure in a tire—See *tire pressure*.
tire pressure	force of the air held in a tire tube
track director	person in charge of the track and the races
two-pedal slip	the slipping of both feet off the pedals while racing
two-pedal start	to stand up on both pedals with front wheel against starting gate
ultra light	*very* lightweight
white lines	lines marking the race track

INDEX